THE MAGIC MIX-UP

Dawn mumbled good-bye and stood there holding the receiver after she heard Danny hang up. A warm tear slowly slid down her cheek. Why had she blurted out that comment about Jennifer? She had sounded so—so *jealous*! How had she let herself become so envious of Jennifer's pretend powers when she had real ones? It would be so simple to let the whole school know about her magic. All she would have to do would be to demonstrate a few tricks of her own.

Dawn felt as though her emotions were tearing her in two directions. One part of her said that a secret as enormous as hers wasn't something to share with the entire world. But the other part of her felt just the opposite. She wanted people like Danny to see what amazing, special powers she had.

The worst part of all was having no idea which of those two things she really wanted.

Other Bantam Skylark Books you will enjoy
Ask your bookseller for the books you have missed

Abracadabra #3

The
Magic
Mix-Up

Eve Becker

A BANTAM SKYLARK BOOK®
NEW YORK · TORONTO · LONDON · SYDNEY · AUCKLAND

RL 5, 009–013

THE MAGIC MIX-UP
A Bantam Skylark Book / December 1989

*Skylark Books is a registered trademark of Bantam Books,
a division of Bantam Doubleday Dell Publishing Group, Inc.
Registered in U.S. Patent and Trademark Office and elsewhere.*

*Produced by Daniel Weiss Associates, Inc.,
27 West 20th Street, New York, NY 10011*

Cover art by Michael McDermott.

Abracadabra is a trademark of Daniel Weiss Associates, Inc.

ISBN 0-553-15770-1

Published simultaneously in the United States and Canada

*Bantam Books are published by Bantam Books, a division of Bantam Dou-
bleday Dell Publishing Group, Inc. Its trademark, consisting of the words
"Bantam Books" and the portrayal of a rooster, is Registered in U.S. Patent
and Trademark Office and in other countries. Marca Registrada. Bantam
Books, 666 Fifth Avenue, New York, New York 10103.*

PRINTED IN THE UNITED STATES OF AMERICA

CWO   0 9 8 7 6 5 4 3 2 1

Abracadabra . . .

It all began on Dawn Powell's thirteenth birthday. That was the day she discovered she could make it snow in the middle of August, clean her room without lifting a finger, or turn tap water into ginger ale. That was the day her grandma Cassie told her about syzygy and how Dawn came to inherit her magical powers.

"Syzygy is when the sun, the earth, and the moon all line up," Grandma Cassie had explained. "It's a very rare phenomenon that disturbs the forces of gravity. Those of us with the power have an old family legend about an ancestor who was born at precisely the strongest moment of this phenomenon. At the time of his birth, there was a

severe electrical storm and a meteorite shower that disrupted the earth's magnetic field.

"In plain English that means that Newbert Charles Caldwell, our many times great-grandfather, came into this world at the very moment when all the Earth's forces were in a state of complete disruption—the split second when the laws of science didn't apply. He later discovered that he had the power to disrupt those forces at will—a power that was passed down through the generations. To us, my dear."

Dawn felt a current of excitement race through her. She had magical powers—and life would never be the same again!

One

Dawn Powell eyed the dirty breakfast dishes piled high in the sink. The kitchen table was littered with cereal boxes and half-finished glasses of juice. An ugly coffee stain was spreading out under the cup and saucer in front of her father's seat. She sighed and picked up the cereal boxes. Why did she always seem to get stuck with cleaning the kitchen on the mornings when she was late for school?

Dawn glanced at her watch. She was supposed to pick up her cousin Jennifer in ten minutes. She would never get there on time. Unless . . .

Well, why not? thought Dawn. Her parents had already left for work and her eleven-year-old brother, Paul, had just rushed off to basketball practice. April, Dawn's older sister, had a date after school, so she was upstairs changing outfits for the fifth time that morning. No one was around to see anything.

Dawn looked at the Raisin Oats and the Toasties boxes in her hands and arched her eyebrow sharply. The boxes floated out of her grasp, sailed across the room, and parked themselves neatly on the shelf above the sink.

She turned and arched her eyebrow at the mess on the table. The milk carton glided toward the refrigerator. The juice glasses and dirty silverware paraded through the air and landed in the sink. In a few moments, the dishes were clean, dried, and in their proper places. The coffee stain on the table was gone. The kitchen sparkled.

Dawn surveyed her handiwork. Just one thing was missing. She arched her eyebrow again and a vase filled with cattails, fresh green ferns, and slender branches with bright red berries appeared in the center of the table. Perfect! Her mother would love the fall bouquet. Thank goodness for magic!

It was hard to believe that only a few months

earlier, Dawn had been without it. But everything had changed the day she had turned thirteen. That was the day she discovered the magical powers she had inherited from her grandmother. That was the day she had realized that she could instantly transport herself to school, or turn the water in the bathroom tap into ginger ale, or make it snow in August—all with the arch of an eyebrow.

Ever since that day she had been practicing her magic and learning how to cast more complicated spells. Of course, she was still learning, so she didn't always get the right results. But today her magic was working perfectly. Dawn grabbed her denim jacket and pulled it on over her skirt and sweater. Glancing quickly in the mirror near the front door, she straightened the headband holding back her straight brown hair. She slung her knapsack over one shoulder. "Bye, April," she called up to her sister. "Have fun with Andy."

"I will," April replied.

"Great. See you." Dawn pulled the front door open and then slammed it shut loudly so that April would hear. And then, instead of leaving the house and starting down the front walk, she simply arched her eyebrow. If anybody had been watching, he or she would have seen Dawn disappear into thin air.

Moments later, Dawn touched down a few blocks away, inside her cousin's bedroom.

Even though they had totally different personalities, the two cousins had been best friends for as long as Dawn could remember. Jennifer's mother had died when she was six, and since then Jennifer had spent a lot of time at the Powells' house, especially when her father was away on one of his archaeological digs. Dawn felt as though she could tell her cousin anything. In fact, Jennifer was the only person in the world, besides Grandma Cassie, who knew about her magical powers.

As Dawn dropped down silently in the hammock that stretched across Jennifer's room, her cousin was leaning over her dresser, poking around in the old cigar box where she kept her jewelry. Jennifer was wearing a long black skirt and an oversized black sweatshirt with a silvery scarf around her neck. Her blond, curly hair was pulled back in a ponytail.

"Well, nothing like dressing the part, Jen!" Dawn

said, as Jennifer clipped on a pair of dangling crystal earrings.

Jennifer whirled around. "Dawn!" she gasped. Abruptly she wiped the expression of surprise from her face. "I knew you were there all along."

"Oh, come off it, Jen!" Dawn laughed.

"No, really. I could sense your presence."

"Jen, don't you think you're taking this whole thing a little too seriously? I know Barbie Davison thinks *you're* the one with the magical powers, but still . . ."

Barbie Davison was one of the nosiest people in the eighth grade, and the biggest gossip at Crestfield Middle School. Not too long ago, Dawn and Jennifer had baked a love potion into some brownies, using a magic recipe. Jennifer had secretly given brownies to a few teachers, and Barbie had later told Dawn that she thought Jennifer had magic powers. Since then, Jennifer hadn't been able to resist encouraging Barbie's suspicions.

Now Jennifer was making a pouty face. "Boy, can't a person have any fun? Besides, Dawn, my magic act is helping me to get noticed for Homecoming Queen. Which reminds me. Wait until you see what I bought." She reached into her canvas shoulder bag, and pulled out a small rectangular box decorated with stars and planets.

"Tarot cards," Dawn read out loud.

"Ta-roe," Jennifer corrected her. "The *t* at the end is silent."

"A deck of cards that predict the future?" Dawn asked.

"Exactly," Jennifer answered. "I got them over at the Glass Palace in the Westridge Mall yesterday. They're selling all kinds of cool things now that it's almost Halloween." She sat cross-legged on the floor and laid a few cards out on the rug. "See, here's the Wheel of Fortune, and the Queen of Cups, and the Fool—he usually goes on the bottom of the deck."

"What do you do with them?" Dawn looked at the brightly colored pictures on the cards. Some were decorated with men or women in funny-looking, old-fashioned clothes. Others were covered with cups or swords or other symbols.

"First you have to think of a question or subject," Jennifer explained. "The cards don't exactly give you an answer, but they show you the pluses and minuses of a situation. Just think how excited the kids at school will be when I read their cards. I'm sure it will win me lots of extra votes. We've got a few minutes if you want me to show you how it's done," she offered.

"Sure," Dawn agreed. "I don't believe that the future can be predicted, but let's do it anyway."

"You know, Dawn, if you don't believe, the cards won't work for you," Jennifer said in an eerie voice. Then she added more seriously, "Just remember, until this summer, you didn't believe in magic, either."

"Okay, Jen, you're right. Go ahead and tell my fortune." Dawn grinned. "Anyway, I'll bet you've been waiting for your first victim ever since you bought those cards."

Jennifer stuck her tongue out at Dawn, but she quickly spilled out the rest of the cards and handed Dawn the deck. "Shuffle the cards while you tell me what you want to know about," she instructed.

Dawn split the deck and mixed one half into the other. "I wonder what's going to happen now that Barbie has this idea that you're magical."

"Is that your question for the cards?" Jennifer asked.

Dawn nodded. She shuffled one final time.

Jennifer took the deck back and tapped it. "The answer is in these top ones," she said. "Ready?"

"Ready," said Dawn.

Jennifer turned over the first card. It showed an old man with a walking stick, and said *The Hermit* at the bottom.

"What does it mean?" Dawn asked eagerly.

"Patience, my dear cousin," Jennifer said with a fake accent. "The all-knowing Madame Jennifer has to take the other cards into account before she can give you a proper reading."

Dawn giggled. "Okay, Madame Jennifer."

As Jennifer turned over the next card, she let out a loud gasp. "Well, wouldn't you just know it! And *you* don't believe the cards are right!" Dawn looked at the card under Jennifer's hand. It was labeled *The Magician*. "That's your distant past or foundation," Jennifer said. "Magic. Your great-great-grandfather what's-his-name who gave you your powers!"

"My many times great-grandfather Newbert

Charles Caldwell," Dawn said slowly. "The first one in our family to have magical powers."

As Jennifer turned over several more cards, Dawn stared at the Magician card and wondered if it really could represent Newbert Charles. "Jen, what do you think it means?"

"Well, as I explained, the Magician represents the past. So maybe it means that Barbie Davison's suspicions are based on your inheritance of magical powers," Jennifer said.

"But, Jen, she thinks *you* have them—not me."

"Right." Jennifer nodded. "She's got the wrong cousin. I think that's why the Hermit card turned up."

"That old guy is supposed to be me?" Dawn asked, making a face.

"Don't worry, Dawn," Jennifer said, laughing. "He only represents you in terms of the question you asked the cards. You see, the Hermit's so busy protecting his secrets that he spends all his time hiding out in his little house in the woods. He doesn't get to use his knowledge."

"You mean you think I don't use my magic

enough because I'm afraid people will find out?" Dawn asked.

"It's not what *I* think," Jennifer insisted. "It's what the cards say. Still, if I had your powers," she added, "I would use them more often. *And* I'd use them to help my friends. For instance, I'd absolutely, positively make sure my favorite cousin and best friend became the next Homecoming Queen of Crestfield Middle School."

The Homecoming Queen was to be elected the following week. Jennifer had been nominated for the honor, along with Wendy Hiller and Barbie Davison. The whole school would vote on which eighth grade girl best represented the spirit of Crestfield Middle School. The winner would be presented at halftime during the Homecoming Game, a football game attended by almost everyone who had ever been a student at Crestfield. Then that night, after the game, the Queen would be crowned in front of the entire student body at the biggest dance of the year.

"Maybe when the school votes next week you *will* become Queen," Dawn said. "*Without* my help."

Jennifer sighed. "I hope so. I really want to be in the spotlight at the Homecoming Dance." She gave Dawn a sly look. "I wish *I* had magical powers."

"So what else can Madame Jennifer tell me?" Dawn asked, anxious to change the subject. Dawn had inherited her powers from her mother's side of the family—not her father's side—and she knew that Jennifer was jealous that the magic didn't run in the side of the family they shared. Jennifer pointed to the card next to the Hermit. "Beware the Queen of Wands," she said. The card showed a blond-haired figure holding what looked like a big, green baseball bat. "Normally she's a friendly, loving person. Someone who understands you."

"You!" Dawn suggested. "Look, she's even got the same color hair."

"I don't think it's me," Jennifer replied.

"This Queen of Wands is upside down. That means she could be someone who gets you into trouble."

"That could be Barbie," Dawn exclaimed.

"But, the card may not represent a person at all," Jennifer added. She paused to check the instruction booklet that had come with the cards. "The Queen of Wands also stands for jealousy or emotions that get out of control."

"Jealousy?" Dawn echoed. "I don't get it. Whose jealousy? Barbie's?"

"Well, the cards work in mysterious ways," Jennifer said. She turned over another card. "Hey, here's some good news. I see the Star in your future. That's someone who may be able to help you."

"With the Queen of Wands?"

"If you play your cards right." Jennifer giggled. "The Star also means inspiration, a good opportunity, or maybe using something you've learned in the past to help you in the future." Jennifer snapped her fingers. "Hey! It makes perfect sense. Someone will inspire you to use your magic"—she pointed to the Magician—"to help with whatever problems the Queen of Wands might cause. And this last card," Jennifer continued, "says you'll do a good job of it, too." The card read *Strength*.

"Really?" Dawn said. "My future doesn't sound so bad after all."

"Better than that," said Jennifer. "I think something exciting is about to happen, Dawn!"

"If Madame Jennifer knows how to read her cards, that is," Dawn said.

"Madame Jennifer begs your pardon," Jennifer said, "but of course she knows what the future brings!"

Dawn giggled. "I bet it'll bring a lecture from Ms. Davenport if we're late for class." She glanced at her watch. "Even girls who can read the future have to be in homeroom by eight-thirty."

Two

"Hey, guys! Did you see this?" Megan Stark raced over to the table where Dawn and Jennifer were seated. She was balancing her lunch tray with one hand and waving a copy of the Crestfield Middle School *Bugle* with the other.

"Oh! The latest issue of the paper!" said Cindy Mitchell, who was sitting, with Sue Flagg, across from Dawn.

Dawn pushed her tray down on the table and slid over to make room for Megan.

"Wait till you see what's in the *People* column," Megan said breathlessly. She spread the *Bugle* across the table and opened it up.

"Hey, Megan, can't it wait?" Jennifer asked. She rescued a tarot card from underneath the newspaper. "I'm trying to read Kitty's cards, and she just got a Wheel of Fortune in her future." Kitty De-Vries sat opposite Jennifer, toying with the Cleveland Indians baseball cap she always wore.

"Jen, I'm sorry to interrupt, but this item in the newspaper is about you!" Megan said.

"It is?" Jennifer looked up, this time with more interest.

"What stunt have you pulled now, Jen?" asked Cindy.

"Boy, Jennifer, you get in the *People* section more than anyone," Sue chimed in. Dawn noticed that Sue was letting her bangs grow out—just like Cindy. *That figures,* thought Dawn. Whenever Cindy did something, Sue usually followed.

Dawn looked back to Megan. "Come on, Megan. Tell us what it says."

"Well, according to this column, an anonymous note was sent to the newspaper," Megan said. "The note reads, and I quote, 'Jennifer Nicholson has strange and eerie powers. Beware!'"

16

Dawn grinned at her cousin. "Oh, no, Jen. The Queen of Wands strikes!"

Jennifer laughed. "Dawn, that was in your cards, not mine."

"Who do you think the note is from?" Megan asked.

"I don't even have to guess," Jennifer answered. "Barbie Davison told Dawn to watch out for me." Jennifer was clearly enjoying all the attention. "She thinks I'm dangerous!"

"Wooo-wooo! I'm scared," Kitty said, with mock terror in her voice.

"Kitty, don't you believe there are certain powers that scientists haven't discovered yet?" Sue asked.

"And that Jennifer has them?" Kitty rolled her eyes. "Tell me another one."

"If you don't believe she can predict the future, then why do you want Jennifer to read your cards?" Sue pointed out.

Kitty looked embarrassed as she glanced at the tarot cards. "That's different. I'm just playing a game. Everyone knows there's no such thing as magic."

"I'm with Kitty," put in Cindy. "Eerie powers—
that's ridiculous!"

Dawn had to bite her lip to keep from laughing
out loud. *If only they knew!* she thought.

"I can't understand why Barbie would send a
note like that," Kitty commented.

"Well, maybe Barbie didn't send it at all," Cindy
said. There was a smug smile on her face. "It's all
starting to make sense."

"Cindy, what are you trying to say?" Jennifer
asked.

"Well, you want to be chosen for Homecoming
Queen, don't you, Jennifer?"

"Yeah, but what does that have to do with anything?"

"I wouldn't be surprised if *you* had planted that
story yourself," Cindy said. "As a publicity gim-
mick."

Jennifer laughed. "Cindy, I don't need to be in
the *Bugle* to be chosen Homecoming Queen."

"Well, then maybe it's another one of your prac-
tical jokes. I think you like the attention."

"Think whatever you want," Jennifer said coldly.

"Jennifer would never do something like that,

Cindy," Dawn said quickly. "And even if she did, why would she mention weird powers? There are plenty of other ways to get publicity." She paused for a second, then added, "And what's so weird about magical powers anyway?"

"Come on, Dawn," said Cindy. "You really believe in magic? Next you're going to be telling us you've seen little green men coming out of flying saucers."

"And old women flying around on broomsticks," Kitty added.

Everyone at the table suddenly got a case of giggles. But Dawn didn't think it was funny at all, and she could tell that Jennifer was feeling the same way.

"Well, the joke's on you," Jennifer said. "Only you don't know it."

"Jen, you've got to be kidding," Kitty said.

"Yeah, I believe in magic about as much as I believe that those tarot cards are suddenly going to come to life," Cindy said.

Dawn's gaze met Jennifer's. She could tell exactly what her cousin was thinking. And it was too tempting an idea to pass up. Dawn fixed her eyes on the tarot cards and quickly recited a poem in her head.

> *If seeing is believing,*
> *They are in for a surprise*
> *When they see the cards in motion*
> *Right before their eyes.*

She arched her eyebrow. The Wheel of Fortune began spinning around and around. The King of Cups winked right at Kitty. The scales on the card labeled *Justice* swung up and down.

Dawn felt laughter welling up inside of her as Kitty's jaw dropped open. Sue grabbed Cindy's arm. Megan let out a yelp.

A split second later, Dawn arched her eyebrow again, and all that lay on the cafeteria table were some ordinary tarot cards.

"D-did you see that?" Sue whispered. Her finger trembled as she pointed to the cards.

"See what?" Dawn asked lightly.

"They moved!"

"It must have been an optical illusion," Kitty said, her voice wavering.

"Yeah, our eyes are playing tricks on us," Megan said, just as unsteadily.

"Or maybe there's more to this magic stuff than anyone will admit," Sue said, staring at Jennifer suspiciously.

Dawn looked around the table at her four friends, and her laughter was replaced by a funny, uncomfortable feeling in her stomach. What had come over her? Usually she was so careful about using her magic.

Dawn hadn't meant to confirm the rumor about Jennifer in the *Bugle*. But in spite of herself, she *had* confirmed it, and now the damage was done.

"Ah, it's the Ace of Gossip!" Jennifer said loudly as Dawn and she were on their way to their lockers after lunch.

Dawn watched Barbie Davison whirl around as they passed her in the hallway.

"Hi, Dawn! Hi, Jennifer!" Barbie said brightly. "Ace of what?"

"I think you heard me," Jennifer said. "My tarot cards don't have an Ace of Gossip, but if there were

21

one, I know it'd be the first card I turned up for you."

"Oh, yes, I heard about those cards," Barbie said. "You certainly are interested in some unusual things, Jennifer."

"Unusual? Don't you mean 'strange and eerie'?" Jennifer asked.

"What?" Barbie responded innocently. "What are you talking about, Jennifer?"

"Barbie, I'm sure you haven't forgotten what you told me on the telephone about Jennifer," Dawn chimed in. "You were convinced that Jennifer had some *weird* powers, and you even told me to keep an eye on her."

"Dawn, you didn't go and give away our secret, did you?" Barbie asked.

"Barbie, if it was such a secret, why did you send that note to the *Bugle*?" Jennifer demanded. "If you have something to say about me, I think you ought to say it to my face."

"I don't know what you two are getting at," Barbie insisted.

"We're talking about a certain item in today's pa-

22

per," Jennifer said. She pulled a copy of the paper out of her canvas bag and handed it to Barbie.

A frown crossed Barbie's face as she read the column to herself. When she was finished she flashed Jennifer one of her phony, concerned looks. "Oh, dear, Jennifer. This is just awful. Who would do something like this?"

"Barbie, isn't it just a little too much of a coincidence that the paper says exactly the same thing that you told me over the phone?" Dawn asked.

"But why would *I* have sent an anonymous note about Jennifer to the paper?" Barbie asked innocently.

"Oh, brother," Jennifer exclaimed. She grabbed Dawn's arm. "Let's go, Dawn." Then she turned back to Barbie for a moment. "Maybe you should take your own advice."

"Excuse me?" Barbie looked confused.

"Well, it might be smart to think twice before you pick on somebody with strange powers. You know what it says in the *Bugle*. 'Beware.'"

As Dawn and Jennifer walked away, Dawn was sure she saw a worried look pass over Barbie's face.

Three

"Hey, Jennifer! I heard you can bring cards to life," Mark Potter called from across the room as Dawn and Jennifer walked into French class. "That must mean what it says about you in the *Bugle* is true!"

"Oh, yeah?" Jennifer shot back with a grin. "Maybe the football team needs a little magical help from me now that you're out with that fractured wrist."

"Jen, nothing can make up for the power in this arm!" Mark teased, holding up his cast. "Not even *your* strange and eerie powers."

"Mark, you'd better watch what you say,"

Wanda Jackson said. "Jennifer might turn you into a toad." She probably thought it was true, too, Dawn thought. Wanda watched more TV than anyone, and she believed everything she saw.

"Boy, if you could *really* do that, you'd be the luckiest," Wendy Hiller said enthusiastically.

"You mean the weirdest!" Mark called.

"Nah, the whole thing's just a hoax," another voice from the back of the room piped up.

It seemed that everyone had an opinion about Jennifer. And as far as Dawn could see, her cousin didn't mind one single bit. She was standing in the middle of the class, twirling one end of her long scarf and answering questions.

"You don't really have strange and eerie powers, do you, Jennifer?" Janie Simon asked. Her thin face looked even paler than usual. "I mean, anyone who can make cards come to life . . ."

"Well, I suppose it depends on what you mean by 'strange and eerie,'" Jennifer answered.

Dawn sighed and walked to her seat. She slipped behind her desk, took out her notebook, and resigned herself to watching The Jennifer Nicholson Show until Mademoiselle Tournier arrived. She let out a little laugh. It was actually quite funny. And she was sure that not one person in the room would ever suspect that *she* was the one with the real powers.

"Jen, do a trick for us," Donna Lee called out.

"A trick? Sure." Jennifer reached into her bag and pulled out her tarot cards.

"Oh, the ones you brought to life at lunch!" Janie Simon said nervously. "Are you going to do it again?"

For a second, Dawn wondered if Jennifer was going to look to her for help. But Jennifer shook her head instead. "A good magician never does the same trick twice, Janie."

Jennifer sat down at the nearest empty desk and began shuffling the cards. Her fingers moved like lightning as she deftly spread the cards, face down, along the inside of one forearm. Then, with a flick of her hand, the cards flipped over, one after another, until all of them were face up.

Gasps of admiration went around the classroom. Dawn even found herself letting out a cry of appreciation. She knew Jennifer had been practicing that trick for a long time.

"Whoa! Maybe she really *is* magical!" Wendy Hiller said.

At Wendy's words, Dawn felt an uncomfortable ache in the pit of her stomach. She wished Mademoiselle Tournier would come in so class would start.

Jennifer went on with her performance. "Pick a card," she said, offering Donna Lee a perfectly fanned deck.

Donna selected a card.

"Aha. The Empress," Jennifer said, taking the card from Donna and holding it up for everyone in class to see. It showed a woman on a throne with a large crown. A pair of purple wings sprouted from her back. "The Empress is a mother symbol," Jennifer said. "She represents female influence and power where children are concerned."

"Maybe I'm going to get a baby-sitting job," Donna said.

"Ah, yes," said Jennifer. Dawn noticed she had slipped into her Madame Fortune Teller voice. "The Empress also stands for a businesswoman. I predict you will find many new customers who will need your baby-sitting services. And now, if you'll just put the card back anywhere in the deck . . ."

Donna did as Jennifer told her. Jennifer did a few more fancy shuffling maneuvers. "Okay, Donna, what's your lucky number?" she asked.

"Three."

"Right." Jennifer put the cards on the desk and tapped the deck three times. When she turned over the third card, Dawn wasn't surprised to see the Empress. This was one of Jennifer's favorite tricks, and Dawn had never seen her do it wrong.

"Well, now are you convinced she's got magical powers?" Wanda Jackson asked Mark Potter.

Mark shrugged. "It's a good trick, I'll say that much."

"Big deal. My cousin can do the same one, and he definitely doesn't have magical powers," Donna said.

"But what about when those cards started moving?" Wanda reminded her. "Can your cousin do that?"

As Jennifer launched into another card trick, Dawn doodled in her notebook. She tried to ignore the feeling in the pit of her stomach, but it was impossible. Jennifer was taking this rumor about her imaginary powers too far. What was worse, Dawn had added to the problem herself by making the tarot card figures come to life.

Dawn wondered what was taking Mademoiselle Tournier so long. Their teacher was usually in class before the second bell. Dawn drew a flower. And then, since everybody was watching Jennifer, she entertained herself by arching her eyebrow at her pen. She took her hand off it, and watched it make loops and swirls all over the page. The ink changed from blue to purple to red, covering the paper with rainbow streaks.

"Oh, my gosh!" Wendy Hiller's shriek pierced the air. "That pen! It's moving by itself!"

Dawn quickly grabbed her pen and crumpled up the sheet of paper. Fear shot through her. She had thought that everyone was watching Jennifer.

"Oh, come on, Wendy," Dawn said in the calmest tone she could manage. "All this talk about strange powers must be getting to you." From the center of the room Jennifer was staring at her with shock. *Why did I do something so dumb?* Dawn asked herself. *What's wrong with me today?*

"*Qu'est ce qui se passe, ici?*" Mademoiselle Tournier came through the door at last. "What's happening here? A tea party? You should be using this time to study for the dictation test. Everyone take a seat, please, and get out a piece of paper."

All the kids in the room raced to their seats. Jennifer picked up her cards and stuffed them into the box.

For once Dawn was glad it was dictation day. It would take everyone's mind off what had just happened and all this talk about magic.

Dawn paced back and forth on the steps outside the main entrance to the school. She shivered slightly in the crisp fall air and checked her watch. What was taking Jennifer so long? School had ended fifteen minutes ago. Finally, Dawn raced up the main stairs and poked her head back inside the building.

At first, all she saw was the usual after-school crowd in the front hall getting ready to leave. But then she noticed that no one was rushing for the door. Instead, they had formed a tight circle around something Dawn couldn't quite make out. She stepped closer.

From the edge of the circle, Dawn could see Jennifer's silvery scarf twirling over the crowd. "And now for my famous disappearing scarf trick," Jennifer announced.

Dawn felt a wave of annoyance. Was this why Jennifer had kept her waiting all this time? *I should have just walked home without her,* Dawn thought.

As Jennifer slowly stuffed her scarf into her fist, everyone in the crowd watched her carefully.

"She's just doing it that way for drama," Dawn heard Mary Beth whisper to Barbie Davison. "All it really takes is a split second. And she can do a lot more than just make a scarf disappear. Right, Barbie?"

Barbie's cheeks colored. "What makes you think I know anything about it, Mary Beth?"

"Well, you said you sent that note to the *Bu*—" Mary Beth glanced at Dawn, then clapped a hand over her mouth. "Ooops, I wasn't supposed to say anything, was I?"

Barbie shot Mary Beth a nasty look. Then she turned to Dawn with her phony smile back in place. "I don't know how she got such a silly idea."

Dawn shrugged casually and smiled back at

Barbie, but they both knew that the truth was out. Barbie had sent the note to the newspaper so that people wouldn't vote for Jennifer for Homecoming Queen.

A murmur went through the crowd as the scarf disappeared into Jennifer's fist, and she turned up an empty palm.

"Where'd it go? Where's the scarf?" someone called out.

Dawn waved at her cousin from the back of the crowd. "Jen?"

"Oh, hi, Dawn," Jennifer said as she came over to her. "I didn't see you. What'd you think of my disappearing scarf?"

"Good trick," Dawn said. "But weren't we supposed to meet fifteen minutes ago?"

"Oh, yeah. I was just on my way out," Jennifer said.

"You mean you're not going to make the scarf reappear?" asked a seventh-grade girl with big, round glasses.

"Yeah, where's the scarf?" the boy next to her demanded.

Jennifer looked at Dawn and shrugged. "Just a

few more minutes, okay? I don't want to disappoint my audience."

Dawn sighed. Jennifer could never resist an audience, especially now that she wanted everyone to notice her for the Homecoming Queen elections. Dawn watched her cousin turn to the seventh-grader. "Sure, I can make the scarf reappear. It's as easy as"—she snapped her fingers and then made a fist. —"abracadabra." She opened her fist the tiniest bit, and with her other hand, pulled out the scarf. It glittered as she shook it out and retied it around her neck.

As everyone clapped and cheered loudly, Dawn felt her anger mounting. There was no way she was ever going to get Jennifer to leave.

Suddenly Dawn had an idea. She closed her eyes and concentrated, then recited a poem to herself.

> *Jennifer's tricks*
> *Are finally done,*
> *When an autumn storm*
> *Makes people run.*

She focused on the front entrance to the school and arched her eyebrow. The heavy glass door swung open. Instantly, a powerful wind rushed into the front hall. Leaves and twigs swirled into the building.

Barbie Davison's copy of the *Bugle* went flying through the air. She gave a little shriek and ran after it. Donna Lee's hat blew right off her head. The wind whistled through the corridor. Jennifer clutched at her scarf.

"Shut the door!" Dawn heard a boy yell. Kids were running in all directions, chasing papers that were sailing through the hall like gliders. Dawn even saw a Frisbee whiz by. Marthe Geisbond was hot on its trail, her tie-dyed skirt flaring out around her.

Dawn arched her eyebrow again. Suddenly it was calm. Leaves fluttered to the floor. Donna Lee found her hat and put it back on. Marthe Geisbond grabbed her Frisbee and stuffed it into her knap-sack.

Dawn watched Jennifer fix her scarf and look around her. Her audience had scattered. The magic show was over.

★ ★ ★

"Okay, time to confess," Jennifer said as the two cousins walked across the town square. "You whipped up that wind that blew into school, didn't you?"

Dawn carefully avoided Jennifer's eyes. "How do you know the wind didn't just get really strong and blow open the door on its own?"

"Oh, come on, Dawn, you don't expect me to believe that," exclaimed Jennifer.

"How would you have known what it was like outside," Dawn shot back, "when you were so busy trying to prove that Barbie's rumor is true?"

For a moment Jennifer just stared at Dawn. "So that's the problem," she said softly. "I should have guessed when the upside down Queen of Wands showed up in your cards this morning."

Dawn gave her cousin a quizzical look. "What are you talking about?"

"Remember?" Jennifer said. "The Queen of Wands stands for jealousy. And I think you're jealous."

"Jealous? Of whom?" Dawn demanded.

"Of me," Jennifer said matter-of-factly. "And of

the fact that everyone in school thinks that I'm the one with the powers."

Dawn couldn't believe what she was hearing. "But I'm the one who can do magic—not you, Jen."

"And maybe deep down you really want everyone to know it."

"Jen, that's not true," protested Dawn.

"Then why were you using your powers so much today?" Jennifer demanded. "You're usually so careful. Aren't you nervous about using them up?"

"I don't know," Dawn mumbled. "I mean, even if I do, they'll come back eventually, just like they have every other time I've overdone it."

"But what if something big happens while you're waiting? Something important. And you can't use your magic? I'm just repeating what you always tell me, you know."

"Well, maybe I've been thinking about that Hermit card and trying to use my powers a little more. After all," Dawn couldn't resist adding, "Madame Jennifer advised it."

"That's true," said Jennifer. "I did advise it. You keep your magic a secret because you're afraid the kids at school are going to think you're weird. But now you're seeing that maybe people will start paying more attention to you instead. I know Barbie thought her rumor would turn people against me, but all it's done is gotten me noticed. And I think that's great—especially with the vote for Homecoming Queen coming up next week."

"But, Jen, *I* don't want any extra attention. I found that out during the popularity spell." Back at the beginning of the school year, when Dawn was first learning how to use her powers, she had accidentally made herself the most popular girl at Crestfield Middle School. She hadn't enjoyed it at all.

"The popularity spell was different," Jennifer said. "Then everyone was noticing you because of magic. But this time, well, this time I think you really want the attention."

"I don't know," Dawn said.

"Then why are you doing all this magic right in front of everybody's eyes?" Jennifer asked again. "And always when I'm in the middle of doing some trick of my own. First you made the cards come to life, then the pen started moving around in French class. After that there was the windstorm. Who knows what'll be next?"

"Nothing will be next," Dawn said, dismissing Jennifer's remark with a wave of her hand. But deep inside she knew she couldn't brush off what her cousin was saying. She *was* coming down with a case of jealousy.

Four

"I can't believe it. People think my own cousin has magical powers," Paul said, helping himself to a huge slice of pecan pie at dinner that night. "And Chuck Graham really believes it, too!"

"Chuck Graham? Is he Bobby Graham's younger brother?" April asked. When Paul nodded, she said, "I wouldn't trust his opinion about anything. If he's anything like his brother, all he thinks about is sports."

"Well, Chuck's the best basketball player in the entire middle school," Paul said, defending his idol. "He can make a jump shot better than anyone."

"Maybe so," April replied. "But who actually

believes in magic?" She pronounced the word *magic* as if it were some kind of virus.

Dawn picked at a few pecans from the top of her dessert. The tight, empty feeling in her stomach had stayed with her all afternoon, and now even her family was talking about magic. She wished she could forget the whole subject for a while. Suddenly the phone rang and April jumped up to answer it. "It's for you, Dawn," she called from the kitchen. "It's a boy."

Dawn felt her face getting hot. "Thanks, April," she said, trying to sound as if it were no big deal. But as she caught her parents exchanging a smile, she knew she hadn't fooled anyone. She rushed into the kitchen.

"Hello?"

"Dawn?"

Dawn recognized Danny Page's voice immediately. "Hi, Danny. How are you? I didn't see you in school today."

"Yeah, I stayed home," Danny explained. "I'm not feeling that great." Now that he had said a few words, Dawn could hear that he had a bad cold.

"I'm sorry. I hope it doesn't have anything to do

42

with our getting caught in the rain over the weekend." She and Danny had gone to the movies on Saturday and gotten stuck in a thunder shower as they were leaving the theater.

"Well, um, if that's what did it, I suppose I don't mind," Danny said. "I really had a good time."

"Me, too," Dawn said, a wave of happiness washing over her.

"My little sister filled me in on everything that happened at school today. She said everybody was talking about your cousin."

The queasy feeling in Dawn's stomach was back in an instant. "Well, she was in the *People* column in the school paper, if that's what you mean."

"Yeah," Danny said. "It's really nutty. I can't believe anyone really thinks Jennifer has magical powers, can you?"

Dawn didn't quite know how to answer. "No, I can't believe it, either. Magic. Ha-ha."

"Well, Jennifer sure is something, though," Danny went on.

"What do you mean?" Dawn asked, not really sure she wanted to hear the answer. Hadn't there been enough talk about Jennifer and her powers today?

"From what Amy told me, Jennifer has convinced a lot of the kids that she really *is* magical. I wonder how she did it."

"I don't know. I guesss you'll have to ask her," Dawn said.

"Amy said she made a scarf disappear into thin air," Danny said. "And then she made it come back."

"Uh-huh," Dawn said flatly.

"It sure would be cool to have a cousin who could do magic."

"I guess."

"And I heard Jennifer's been predicting everyone's future with cards," Danny continued. "Does she really know how to do that?"

"She says she does." Dawn wondered if they would ever get off the subject of Jennifer.

"Maybe she could tell my fortune sometime," Danny said. "I'd like to know if I'm going to help the football team win this season."

"Listen, if you want to have your fortune told, maybe you should call Jennifer." The second the words were out of her mouth, Dawn wished she could take them back. But it was too late.

"Oh," Danny said curtly. "If that's the way you feel."

"Wait, Danny, I didn't mean it that way."

"Sure. Well, I've got to go. I guess I'll see you sometime."

Dawn mumbled good-bye and stood there holding the receiver after she heard Danny hang up. A warm tear slowly slid down her cheek. Why had she blurted out that comment about Jennifer? She had sounded so—so *jealous*! How had she let herself become so envious of Jennifer's pretend powers when she had real ones? It would be so simple to let the whole school know about her magic. All she would have to do would be to demonstrate a few tricks of her own. And whammo! Instant attention. Then Danny Page would *really* be impressed.

Dawn felt as though her emotions were tearing her in two directions. One part of her said that a secret as enormous as hers wasn't something to share with the entire world. But the other part felt just the opposite. She wanted people like Danny to see what amazing, special powers she had.

The worst part of all was having no idea which of those two things she really wanted.

Five

"I can picture it now!" Jennifer cried excitedly the next morning before school. "A magical team!" She wrapped a scarf around her head, covering the lower part of her face. "Draped in mystery, they roam the American landscape, creating adventure wherever they go. It's the incredible cosmic cousins!"

Dawn giggled. "They vanish in a cloud of magical dust and no one knows where they'll strike next!"

"What a great idea, Dawn! If you do decide to tell everyone about your magic, we'll be Crestfield Middle School's most famous pair."

Suddenly Dawn felt a twinge of nervousness. "You know, it's pretty funny to think about it, and we might have a good time at first. But maybe telling everyone about my magic isn't such a good idea. Even if I have been acting a little jealous," she added apologetically.

"But, what about Danny, Dawn?"

"Well, I would be lying if I said I didn't care what he thought." Dawn could feel her face turning pink. "But, Jen, I want him to be my friend for me. Not for my magic. I mean, him and everyone else at school, too. Do you know what I mean?"

"No, I don't. I can't understand why you'd want people to think you're just exactly like everyone else. I mean, talk about bo-ring!"

How could she make Jennifer understand? "Look, Jen, I'm afraid people might get the idea that I don't have feelings like everybody else. I don't want them to think that I'm not, I don't know, not normal or something."

"You think having magical powers is normal?"

Dawn could feel her face growing warmer. "Jennifer, are you purposely trying to make this harder for me than it already is? My powers are the greatest, most wonderful thing in the world. I just don't know if I'm ready to go public with them, all right?"

Instantly, Jennifer looked sorry. "I didn't mean to get you all upset, Dawn. It's just that it would be so great to be a magical team at school. Anyway, it was your idea."

"Well, now I'm not so sure it was a good one. But I'll keep thinking about it," Dawn said, not wanting to hurt her cousin's feelings. "In the meantime, you go ahead and be as magical as you want," she added. "You were right. It wasn't fair of me to break up your magic act yesterday. I promise. I'm through being jealous."

"Are you sure, Dawn? If you really don't want me to practice any more of my tricks at school . . ."

For a second, Dawn was tempted to take Jennifer up on her offer. But it wouldn't be fair. "Jen, you've worked hard on your tricks. There's no reason you shouldn't show them to all the kids at school, especially if it will get you Homecoming votes. Speaking of which, weren't you going to show me your Homecoming outfit? We still have about twenty minutes before we have to leave for school."

"Oh, Dawn, wait till you see it!" Jennifer raced over to her closet, dodging the clothes that littered the floor. When she opened the closet door, several mismatched shoes came spilling out. She buried her hands in the jumble of shirts and skirts hanging on the rack, and pulled out what she was looking for.

"Oh, Jen!" Dawn felt her breath catch as Jennifer held up the dress. The golden threads woven through the cream-colored silk gleamed in the sunlight. The sleeves billowed gently, and the full skirt hung down to the floor in soft folds. "It's absolutely beautiful. Like a ball gown from another time."

Jennifer nodded. "That's exactly what it is. I found it in a trunk in the attic. Dad says it belonged to my great-grandmother. And guess what? It fits me perfectly." Jennifer held the dress up to herself. "Is it perfect for the Homecoming Queen, or what?"

"It's definitely regal-looking," Dawn agreed. "You've got to win, Jen. You sure are going to look great." Dawn reached out and touched the shiny fabric. "Will you try it on for me?"

"Will you try it on for me, *Your Highness,*" Jennifer said, with mock sternness.

"Oh, of course. Your Highness," Dawn said. She giggled as she dropped a little curtsy in front of her cousin.

"Well, when you put it that way . . ." Jennifer quickly stepped out of her clothes, and Dawn helped her into the gown. "Wow! Make room for Her Majesty." She took a step backward for a better look. The color of the dress looked perfect with Jennifer's blond hair.

Jennifer twirled around to give Dawn the full effect. The dress made a swishing sound as it brushed her bare feet. "You didn't find a pair of shoes that matched in that trunk, did you?"

"Unfortunately not," Jennifer said. "And I can't imagine finding the right ones in the Crestfield Mall."

Dawn shook her head. "No. They'd need to be old-fashioned, or they'd look out of place. They should be gold, like the dress, and good for dancing."

"Definitely. So maybe I should be wearing little ballet slippers—"

"—made out of gold brocade," Dawn finished. "I can picture exactly what they look like. In fact—" She arched her eyebrow, and suddenly Jennifer had the delicate slippers on her feet.

"Oh, Dawn! They're absolutely, positively perfect!" Jennifer waltzed across the carpet and gave Dawn a hug. "Thanks so much."

"I couldn't resist," Dawn said. "You just look so incredible. You know, I like seeing you looking romantic, for once."

Jennifer stopped in her tracks. "Romantic? Ugh!"

"Come on, Jen. You look like a queen, exactly as you should," Dawn reminded her. "Go over to the mirror and take a look at yourself."

Jennifer's skirt swished as she walked toward the mirror on the back of her closet door. Just as she got there, Dawn arched her eyebrow again. "Long live the queen!" she called. A crown of sparkling jewels appeared on her cousin's head.

Jennifer gasped as she stared at her reflection. "Wow, this is even better than my crystal earrings," she said. "Hey, I just realized something. We haven't decided on what *you're* going to wear."

"Me?" Dawn said.

"Sure. When I get chosen Homecoming Queen, you're going to be my lady-in-waiting." Dawn could feel her cousin's gaze on her. "I know! You'll be wearing a dress just like mine, only a deep rose, to go with your dark hair."

Dawn laughed. "Well, I guess it's my duty to obey my queen." She got up and stood next to Jennifer, looking at herself in the mirror. The girl who looked back was tall and skinny, and dressed in jeans and a sweater. At least until she arched her eyebrow.

Dawn felt the heavy folds of silk fall around her legs as her jeans and sweater melted into yards of deep rose fabric. Her satin ballet flats matched the color of the dress exactly. Dawn had to admit it: the girl who stared back at her in the mirror looked very pretty.

"Way to go!" Jennifer said approvingly. "That's the perfect shade for you. Now all we need is a carriage and two white horses!" she joked.

In an instant Dawn was reciting a poem:

> *A snow white horse*
> *Befitting a queen,*
> *With a bridle of gold,*
> *Will appear on the scene!*

In the arch of an eyebrow, a loud whinnying split the air. Even Dawn jumped as the white stallion materialized on the carpet. His saddle was gold, with a raised *J* on it for Queen Jennifer. He looked like something out of a storybook.

For once, Jennifer was totally speechless.

"Sorry, Jen, but two horses and a carriage wouldn't fit in the room," Dawn said.

Suddenly, the door flew open.

"Girls! What's going on in there?"

"Ginger!" Jennifer gasped. Ginger was a student of Jennifer's father at the university, and she helped out with the cooking and cleaning around the Nicholsons' house. Somehow, she always managed to show up at exactly the wrong moment.

"Oh, my heavens!" Ginger's voice trembled. "There's a horse in this room." Beneath her freckles, the color drained from her face.

Dawn arched her eyebrow quickly. The horse was gone. She arched her eyebrow again. Her beautiful ball gown turned back into her plain jeans and top. Jennifer's crown disappeared right off her head. The only thing Dawn didn't get rid of were the golden slippers. Where else was Jennifer ever going to find that kind of match for her great-grandmother's dress?

"A horse?" Dawn said calmly to Ginger. "What are you talking about?"

"Really!" Jennifer joined in. "A horse? In my bedroom?" She tried to look amazed. "How could a horse ever fit up the staircase? Ginger, are you all right?"

Ginger didn't budge from the doorway. "Just wait until your father hears about this, young lady," she said. "This time, I'm going to tell him everything."

"You're going to tell him there was a horse in my bedroom?" Jennifer shook her head. "Ginger, I hope you're planning to take a really long vacation during your winter break. I think you need it." She turned to Dawn. "A horse. Right here in my room. Can you believe it?"

Dawn struggled to keep a straight face. Poor Ginger.

Ginger sighed. "How come whenever you two are together weird things always happen? There's something fishy going on. I was sure I heard a— oh, never mind." Ginger turned to leave. But then she spun on her heel to take one last look, as if she expected the horse to reappear.

As soon as Ginger's footsteps echoed on the wooden staircase, Jennifer shut her bedroom door and the two cousins burst into laughter.

"I know you think I should let the whole world know about my powers, Jen," Dawn said, when she was finally able to stop laughing. "But it's times like this that make keeping it our secret much more fun!"

Six

Dawn was dialing the combination to her gym locker when she heard someone mention her cousin's name.

"Jennifer Nicholson?" said a voice from the other side of the row of lockers. "Nah, I don't think she's the best choice," the girl continued. Dawn instantly recognized Liza Martin's voice. She spoke louder than anyone else in the eighth grade.

"But, Liza, she's magic," said a different voice. "Don't you think it would be neat to have a Homecoming Queen like that?"

Dawn felt a tug in her stomach. Liza was talking to Wanda Jackson.

"Wanda, you've got to get out of this habit of believing every single thing you hear," Liza said in her most mature tone. "Life is not one big TV show."

"You mean you don't believe Jennifer's got strange powers?" Wanda said. "Then how did she make those cards come to life?"

She means, *How did I make those cards come to life,* Dawn thought. Maybe Jennifer was right. Maybe the only way she was going to stop feeling jealous was to let the whole world know what Dawn Powell could really do.

"Well, I didn't see any cards move," Liza said. "I mean, I wasn't even there. Were you?"

"No, but Cindy Mitchell told me about it. And anyway, you've seen some of the other stuff she can do, haven't you?"

"Well, I did see her make her scarf disappear," Liza admitted.

"So," Wanda said eagerly, "you don't think it's out of the question that the rumor is true."

"Look, Wanda," Liza said loudly, "the point isn't whether or not I believe Jennifer Nicholson can do magic. The point is that she wants people to believe it, whether it's true or not. She likes being weird. She's purposely not acting normal. And that's not my idea of a Homecoming Queen. The queen's supposed to be a typical Crestfield girl with a lot of spirit. And I'm not the only one who thinks so. I've been talking to plenty of kids who feel the same way."

Dawn felt her jealousy vanish. Plenty of kids thought Jennifer was weird? That was exactly what Dawn was afraid people would say about *her* if they found out about her powers. Now telling everyone about her powers seemed a lot less important than it had this morning. Thank goodness she hadn't let her secret out!

"Yeah, I guess you're right," Wanda said. "I mean, I still think Jennifer's tricks are really neat, but I suppose the queen should be someone, well, like a regular person."

Dawn sank down on the bench in front of her locker. Poor Jennifer! All this time her cousin had thought her magic act was winning her votes. Instead it was only making some of the kids at school less likely to elect her.

"So, if you're not voting for Jennifer, who are

you going to vote for?" Dawn heard Wanda ask Liza.

"Well, Wendy Hiller might make a good Homecoming Queen," Liza answered. "I mean, she *is* the football team's biggest fan. Although she goes a little overboard, sometimes. I wonder if she does the Cougar cheer in her sleep. But anyway, I guess when you really get down to it, the person who's most involved with the school is Barbie Davison."

Dawn felt her mood dive even lower. Barbie, again? It was her fault that the rumor about Jennifer had spread in the first place. This was probably exactly what Barbie had been counting on when she'd planted that item in the *Bugle*. All the talk about Jennifer's being weird would edge her right out of the Homecoming competition.

"I heard Barbie's giving a Halloween party for the entire eighth grade class," Liza continued. "I mean, how much more involved can you get than that?"

A party for over a hundred kids? *Well, that's certainly one way to win votes,* Dawn thought. Especially when your father is the head of Toasties

Cereal and you live in a mansion big enough to hold everybody.

"So, we're voting for Barbie?" Wanda asked.

"We're voting for Barbie," Liza agreed.

Dawn stood up with a sigh and finished opening her locker. It was a sad thought, but maybe she wasn't going to see her cousin on the throne at Homecoming after all.

"Janie, would you like to verify the fact that this can is absolutely, positively, empty?" Jennifer asked.

"Me?" Janie Simon said nervously, as Jennifer handed her the ordinary-looking pineapple juice can. Janie peered inside as if something were going to jump out and bite her. "Well, it looks empty," she said. She turned it upside down and shook it to make certain. "Yeah, I guess it is." She nodded.

"Jennifer?" Dawn approached the little group that had gathered outside the cafeteria doors.

Jennifer took the can back as her eyes met Dawn's. "Hey, Dawn, you're just in time to see the famous empty can trick."

"I've seen that trick before. I need to talk to you right away," she said.

"As soon as I'm finished," Jennifer said. She had on another long, black outfit today. This one was a narrow dress that flared at the very bottom.

"Um, Jen, it's important," Dawn said.

"Dawn, you don't want to mess up my trick purposely, do you?" Jennifer asked, fastening the lid onto the can. "Yesterday you promised . . ."

Dawn sighed. That was true. She had told Jennifer she wouldn't interfere with any more of her magical demonstrations. Still, if enough of their classmates felt like Wanda Jackson and Liza Martin, every trick Jennifer did meant a few less votes she could count on for Homecoming Queen. But a promise was a promise.

Dawn watched Jennifer pass her free hand over the can and mumble a string of nonsense words. Then she yanked the top off. Yard upon yard of brightly colored streamers popped out of the can and spilled onto the floor.

"Ooo," Janie exclaimed. "What a neat trick!" The nervousness on her face melted into admiration.

"Now, Jennifer?" Dawn said. She didn't want to

give Jennifer a second opportunity to start another trick.

"Oh, okay." Jennifer picked up the streamers and stuffed them into the can. "I'll show you more later," she said. "And don't forget, everybody. This Homecoming is going to be a magical evening!" Her smile rested for a moment on each of her classmates before she turned and joined Dawn. Dawn quickly led her cousin down the hall.

"Hey, why are we going into Mademoiselle Tournier's classroom?" Jennifer asked as Dawn pushed open the door.

"Because no one's in here," Dawn said. "I have something important to tell you."

Suddenly Dawn saw Jennifer's face light up. "Oh, Dawn! This is going to be the best!"

"It is?" Dawn asked, giving her cousin a quizzical look.

"Sure. Now I understand why you couldn't wait to talk to me." Jennifer jumped up and down. "You're going to tell everyone about your powers! This will be so great!"

"Oh." Dawn sat down on the nearest desk top. "Jen, you've got it all wrong."

"I do?" Jennifer's face fell. "Then what? Don't tell me you're still jealous. You want me to quit doing tricks, don't you?"

"Yes, Jen. I think you should take a break from your tricks for a while. Just until Barbie's rumor dies down. But it's not because I'm jealous."

"It's not? Then why do you want to put a stop to my campaign for Homecoming Queen?"

"Because your magic tricks aren't winning you any votes. They're doing exactly the opposite."

"You *are* still jealous," Jennifer said, giving Dawn a suspicious look.

"Jen, I was jealous of all the attention you've been getting, but I'm not anymore. I heard something in the girls' locker room that changed everything." Dawn repeated the conversation she had overheard earlier that day.

Jennifer sank into a chair. "Well, why didn't you tell me before I went and did that dumb can trick just now?"

"I tried to," Dawn said.

"Oh. I guess you did." Jennifer didn't say anything for a moment. "Well, maybe that's just Wanda and Liza. I still have plenty of fans. Did you see the expression on Janie Simon's face when those streamers came popping out?"

"Jen, that doesn't mean she's going to vote for you," Dawn said. "Can't you see you scare her half to death? Besides, Liza said there are plenty of other kids who feel the same way she does."

Dawn couldn't stand to see Jennifer looking so unhappy. "But that doesn't mean it's all gloom and doom," she added quickly. "Your best friends will all vote for you. Magic or not, you know you can count on us."

But Jennifer's expression just got darker. "I might as well tell you," she said. "Kitty thinks I'm a huge fake. She says she doesn't even want to sit near me at lunch anymore. And Cindy claimed that I got on the volleyball team by magic. So I told her to go jump in a lake. I don't think she'll be voting for me. Which means Sue won't be either, of course."

"Oh. How come you didn't tell me any of this before?" Dawn asked. "And why didn't you stop doing your tricks right away?"

"I don't know." Jennifer's voice wavered. "I guess I had myself convinced that it didn't matter.

Until right now, I thought being magic was going to get me so many votes that Kitty and Cindy wouldn't make a difference."

"But, Jen, Kitty's your best friend. I mean, after me."

Jennifer nodded miserably. "Yeah, but I was just so mad that she didn't believe I was magical. Even though there's no reason why she should."

Dawn felt terrible. Jennifer wanted to have powers so badly.

"Listen, Dawn, suppose I wanted to stop all the rumors about me. I mean, I'm not saying I really want to," she added quickly, "but what if? Could you arrange it so that everyone forgets they ever read that business Barbie managed to get printed in the *Bugle*?"

Dawn bit her lip. "Jen," she said finally, "that *People* column is written in history."

"So? Can't you un-write it?"

"I wish I could," she said softly. "But you know it's impossible to change history. Even with magic. I could try from now till next summer, and I wouldn't be able to undo what's happened in the past couple of days. I'm sorry, Jen."

"Oh. Well, don't be. I don't care what Wanda and Liza think anyway." Jennifer managed a smile. But Dawn could tell that it was emptier than her famous empty can.

Seven

"Danny!" Dawn summoned up her courage and raced after him in the hallway. She'd been looking for him all afternoon. "Hey, Danny!"

Danny turned around. "Oh, hi, Dawn," he said flatly.

"How're you feeling?" she asked.

"Well, I'm in school," Danny answered.

"So I guess that means you're better," Dawn said brightly. "Listen, Danny, about the way I acted on the phone last night—"

Danny waved his hand. "Hey, don't worry about it. I'm not asking for an explanation."

"But I want to explain. I guess I got a little jealous of all the attention Jennifer's been getting since that note about her appeared in the *Bugle*. Then when you called, well, it was just one person too many that day who wanted to talk about her. You know what I mean?"

Danny's expression softened. "Yeah, I guess it's hard having a magician in the family."

"Right, it can be hard sometimes," she replied. "So I'm sorry that I snapped at you."

Dawn heard someone step up behind them.

"Well, hello, you two!" said Barbie Davison. With her were Cindy Mitchell and Liza Martin.

Barbie turned her hundred-watt smile on Danny. "You're coming to my Halloween party, aren't you?" Then she glanced at Dawn. "Oh, I guess you're invited too, Dawn."

"I wouldn't miss it for anything, Barbie," Dawn muttered.

Barbie was all phony sweetness. "Wonderful. It's going to be so much fun. I've got my costume all planned out already."

Dawn didn't ask what it was, but Barbie told her anyway. "I'm going to be a cowgirl," she said. "I have all the authentic gear from my summer on the dude ranch—the boots and hat, even a lasso. Did you know I won a blue ribbon in calf roping?" she asked, looking right at Danny.

"Well, isn't that terrific?" Dawn said, making her voice as bright and cheery as Barbie's.

"Oh, I just can't wait," Barbie said. "Your cousin will be coming, too, won't she, Dawn?"

"Are you kidding?" Liza Martin shrieked. "Halloween is Jennifer Nicholson's favorite holiday! Ghosts and spooks and all kinds of weirdos just like her. Yuck!"

Dawn felt her face turning red. How dare Liza Martin insult her cousin!

"Aw, come on, Liza," Danny said lightly. "You just wish you were as original as Jennifer."

"Well, the two-headed woman in the circus is original, too," Liza retorted. "And you wouldn't catch me trading places with her." Cindy laughed along with Liza.

"Jennifer Nicholson is a menace to this school," Liza went on. "She ought to get on her broomstick and fly off to Darkside Middle School, or wherever the rest of her kind are."

Dawn was getting angrier by the second. How

could they say such horrible things about Jennifer, or about anyone with magical powers? *Liza Martin doesn't know anything,* Dawn thought, *she should button her lip.*

Dawn eyed the oversized, white buttons that went down the front of Liza's blouse, and pictured one of them right smack in the middle of her mouth. That was exactly what Liza deserved. Her anger churning inside her, Dawn's left eyebrow twitched sharply.

Before she had realized what she had done, a big white button appeared on Liza's lips. Liza tried to say something, but she couldn't get her mouth open. All that was coming out through her closed lips was a muffled squeak.

Cindy Mitchell began laughing hysterically. But it was Barbie Davison's scream that brought Dawn back to reality. Oh, no! She had just cast another spell in plain view of everyone. Frantically, she arched her eyebrow again. The button vanished. Liza's squeal turned into an open-mouthed wail.

Dawn tried to stay calm, but her heart was racing. Danny's face was pale. "What's the matter, Liza?" Dawn asked weakly.

Barbie Davison whirled toward Dawn, for once

not even bothering to smile. "You know what's the matter," she said in a whisper. "I should have known all along. I heard about your pen moving around by itself in French class. And I saw that wind storm inside school with my very own eyes."

"Barbie, what are you talking about?" Dawn asked, trying to sound as innocent as she could.

"I'm talking about the way you buttoned Liza's lip," Barbie said. "And all the other funny business you've been up to. I don't know why I didn't see it right away. It must run in the family! You've got those powers, too!"

Dawn felt icy cold, from the tips of her toes to the end of her ponytail. Barbie was on to her. And she had witnesses, too. Dawn could feel Liza Martin staring at her in terror. Cindy Mitchell's jaw hung open in amazement. Dawn turned to Danny, desperately hoping he would stick up for her again, and somehow save her from this terrible mess. But Danny just stood there, with a look of confusion in his eyes.

Dawn could feel the tears welling up inside her. Just when she had discovered how important it was to guard her secret, she had let her emotions get the better of her. Now the entire school was going to be talking about how strange and eerie she was.

As she felt the first sting of tears on her cheeks, she started racing blindly down the hallway. She had to get away. But in the back of her mind, a little voice was telling her she couldn't escape the horrible truth. She had given away her most important secret in the whole world.

"Dawn! Wow, I heard some pretty cool news," Donald McNeil said, stopping her a little while later as she was about to go into her Social Studies class. "Boy, you sure are lucky."

"I am?" Dawn couldn't believe how quickly word had gotten around Crestfield Middle School. "You shouldn't believe everything you hear, Donald."

"Yeah, right." Donald gave her a sly wink. "Now I understand how you manage to be at the top of the honor roll every marking period. Some people get all the breaks."

Dawn felt her cheeks growing warm. "Donald McNeil! I did not get on the honor roll by cheating, if that's what you're trying to say!"

"Hey, it's okay. I'd do it exactly the same way, if I could. In fact, if you want to do me a little favor . . ."

Dawn held her breath and slowly counted to ten. Then she said, "Donald, I got on the honor roll by working hard. And doing all my homework. If you want to get on the honor roll, I'd suggest that you do the same."

"Oh," Donald said flatly. "Gee, some people don't like to spread their luck around, do they?"

Dawn turned and marched into the classroom.

"Well, if it isn't Miss Magic, number two," Marthe Geisbond called out. Dawn spotted her in the back of the room, not too far from Megan. Her frizzy hair was tucked under a tie-dyed scarf. "Hey, Dawn, how are tricks?"

Dawn managed a weak little "Hi."

"Boy, couldn't you have thought up something a little more original instead of just copying your cousin?" Donna Lee said.

"That's the point," Janie Simon told Donna. "Their spooky powers run in the family." As Dawn passed her desk, Janie leaned away, as if she were trying to get as far from Dawn as possible.

"Family, my eye," Donna answered. "There's no such thing as magic. This is just some new gag Jennifer cooked up. Believe me. Jennifer's on the volleyball team with me, and I know how she is."

"Hey, Dawn! Will you tell my fortune?" Marthe yelled across the room.

"Sorry, Marthe. I don't know how to predict the future," Dawn answered. She had never felt so misunderstood in her life.

Megan flashed her a sympathetic smile from her seat across the aisle. "Don't mind them," she whispered. "You know how it is around here. This whole thing will fade away when the next rumor hits."

Dawn nodded. But she couldn't get herself to feel as optimistic as Megan sounded. All those other rumors had died out because they were lies. But this one was different. This rumor was the truth.

Eight

"What a great hideout!" Jennifer said. She reached out and picked a ripe red apple from the branch nearest her perch.

"Yeah, the secret headquarters of Crestfield Middle School's magical duo," Dawn said, trying to joke off everything that had happened that afternoon. Actually, it was hard to stay upset too long up here. They were sitting in the wide yoke of the tallest apple tree in all of Haight's Orchard. Trees dripping with fruit spread out in all directions. On one side, the orchard gave way to a blaze of orange and amber leaves, burning with fall color. On the other, far in the distance, she could see a tiny, shimmering strip of Lake Erie. It was a great place to go to get away from people. And right now was definitely one of those times when she wanted to be alone.

"The magical duo," Jennifer echoed. "Boy, I can't believe that just this morning I thought that was the greatest idea."

"Well, you got your wish," Dawn said.

"Great. Now that I don't want it any more," Jennifer said. "Once you told me about Liza and Wanda, I started thinking more about the way everyone reacted. You were right. I think my entire audience is going to turn around and vote for Barbie Davison. And you know, I bet she's the one spreading it around that I got my gymnastics trophy by magic." Jennifer frowned. "Boy, I'd like to see *her* try and do a double flip into a split."

"It's the same with me," Dawn sympathized. "Donald McNeil was telling everyone in our Social Studies class that I used my magic to get on the honor roll."

"Boy, the way people are acting," said Jennifer, "they'd deserve it if we went and cast a big spell on all of them."

"You're not serious, Jen."

"Think about it, Dawn. We could turn all the alligators upside down on Cindy Mitchell's alligator shirts. We could make Gary Elwood mess up simple addition or subtraction problems. Or fix it so goody-goody Mary Beth Carter gets an uncontrollable desire to talk back to her teachers."

Dawn giggled. "Lucky for everyone at school that you *don't* have magical powers."

"Yeah, but you have them."

"No way, Jen," said Dawn. "I don't think that's the answer, even if it would be funny. The only way we're going to get ourselves out of this mess is to convince everyone that the rumors about us just aren't true."

"But if we can't unwrite that *People* column in the newspaper, what are we supposed to do?"

Dawn reached out and picked an apple off one of the branches. "I wish I had an answer," she said. "If only I hadn't gotten so jealous. And then I got so mad at big mouth Liza Martin, I fouled things up even more."

"Hey, I'm the one who wanted everyone to believe the rumor in the first place," Jennifer said. "I just couldn't help trying to pretend I really did have powers. You know, it's what I've been dreaming about ever since you told me about yours. I suppose in my own way, I was acting as jealous as you were."

Dawn took a bite of her apple. "I don't suppose it matters whose fault it is, anyway," she said with a sigh. "I wish we could stay here forever and never face anyone at school again. But the fact is, we're in it together. And we're going to have to figure out a way to get out of it together."

Jennifer finished the last bite of her apple, and tossed away the core. "Yeah, but how do you go about stopping a rumor at school?"

"I wish I knew, Jen," Dawn answered softly.

"I'm going to be an astronaut for Halloween," Paul announced at dinner. He put some brussels sprouts on his plate and passed Dawn the bowl. "I finally decided."

"Well, then you won't need a disguise," April said. "You're in outer space to begin with."

"Very funny," Paul said. "What are you going as, anyway?"

"I'm too old to dress up for Halloween," April said.

"Nonsense," Mr. Powell said. "Your mother and I were invited to a party over at the Pages, and we're wearing costumes, aren't we, sweetheart."

Mrs. Powell put a chicken wing on her plate. "Your father is going as Romeo, and I'm dressing up as Juliet."

"A tall, raven-haired, beautiful Juliet," Mr. Powell said. "Only this Romeo and Juliet have a happy ending." He leaned over and gave his wife a kiss.

Paul let out a groan. "That is the dumbest, mush-iest thing I've ever heard. Romeo and Juliet?"

"I think it's sweet," April said. "As long as you're going to get dressed up, that is."

"And what are you going as, Dawn?" her mother asked. "We haven't heard a peep out of you all evening."

"I don't know yet," Dawn said.

"But, dear, Halloween is in a few days."

"Gee, honey," her father added, "this isn't like you. You usually love thinking up original costumes. What was it you went out as one year? A baby?"

"A baby in a blanket," Mrs. Powell added. "She wore a nightgown, held a rattle and carried the big basket we use for firewood. Every time she rang

81

someone's doorbell she put the basket down and climbed in."

Mr. Powell chuckled. "Well, I guess you're busy thinking up something to top that one, huh, sweetheart?"

Dawn shrugged. The truth was, she'd been too busy thinking about how to put an end to the rumors at school to give much thought to Halloween.

"Dawn, are you feeling all right?" asked her mother.

"I feel fine," Dawn said, but her voice didn't come out sounding very convincing.

"I know," Paul said. "You're in a bad mood because everyone at school's teasing you about having weird powers."

"Didn't you tell us last night that Jennifer was the magical one?" Mr. Powell said with a wide grin. "Since when are both of you magic?"

Dawn opened her mouth to protest, but Paul interrupted her. "Actually, Dad, it's not funny. All this dumb talk about Dawn and Jennifer cost me some serious points in basketball practice today."

"Dumb talk?" April asked. "Yesterday you said you believed that Jennifer really was magical."

Paul glared at April. "I said Chuck Graham believed it. And I don't think Chuck's as great as I used to think he was."

"What happened?" Dawn asked, almost afraid to hear the answer.

"Well, the coach decided it would be good for us if the J.V. played a practice game against the varsity team. And I was really psyched because I got to cover Chuck. Anyway, the game starts, and I'm playing great. Only instead of getting respect, I hear Chuck start mumbling about how it's all because of my magic. He's telling everyone that my sister has it, and my cousin has it, and that I must, too, because it runs in my family. Me, magic! Have you ever heard anything so crazy?"

Dawn bit her lip. Whenever Paul got worked up, his left eyebrow arched furiously in a way that reminded Dawn of herself. Her grandmother had told her that Paul was the only other person in her family who might inherit powers, too, on his thirteenth birthday.

"Magic! Hah!" April said. "The things you guys come up with."

"Yeah, it's pretty wild," Paul said. "But the most amazing part was that after I scored a few baskets, and Chuck made a few more comments, half the guys on both teams believed him. Chuck called me a cheater and said that he was going to wait for me after school and teach me a lesson."

Mrs. Powell gave him a startled look. "Oh, no, Paul. You didn't get into a fight, did you?"

"No way, Mom," Paul answered. "Chuck is huge. I decided the only way to get everyone off my back was to play badly on purpose and prove that what Chuck was saying wasn't true." Paul frowned. "I think maybe I overdid it. I mean, making those bad shots and passes really hurt."

"But it worked?" Dawn asked. She was getting an idea.

"After that, they left me alone. Chuck was the big hero of the game, and he took back everything he'd said. He even told me that my first quarter playing showed great potential."

"Chuck was the hero, huh?" Dawn mused aloud. That was it! What a great idea! She had the solution to her problem and Jennifer's! She wolfed down the rest of her dinner and pushed her chair away from the table. "Mom? May I be excused?"

"Well, you certainly changed moods quickly," her mother said. "Don't you want any dessert? I bought that new flavor of ice cream you like so much."

"Macadamia Swirl? Great. I'll save mine for later." Dawn stood up. "Listen, is it okay if I go over to Jennifer's for a while?"

"Is all your homework done?" her father asked.

Dawn nodded. "All except for a little bit of reading for Ms. D's class. But I can finish it up when I get back."

"All right, then," Mr. Powell said.

"Thanks," Dawn said.

"Off to cook up some kind of magical brew?" April teased.

"No, that was a few weeks ago," Dawn said. "Jennifer and I concocted a love potion. That's why you and Andy are so happy together." She swallowed a giggle. What on earth would April say if she found out that Dawn was telling the truth?

"For your information, Andy and I are happy together because we were made for each other," April said with a blissful little sigh.

"That, too," Dawn agreed. "Bye, everyone." She flashed Paul an extra special smile. He had really helped her out. "Good-bye, my wonderful brother."

"Huh?" Paul called after Dawn as she raced out of the dining room. "You may not have magical powers, but I think you have a screw loose upstairs."

"Paul!" Dawn heard her father scold.

Normally, Dawn would have tried to think up a good comeback for her little brother. But tonight, she didn't mind him at all. She made a promise to herself that as soon as the rumors died down, she would make sure Paul scored enough baskets to more than make up for the ones he had missed that afternoon.

"Hi, Uncle Kenneth!" Dawn gave her uncle a big hug. His bushy, salt and pepper beard tickled her cheek. "Hi, Ginger!" she called out, sticking her head into the study.

Ginger looked up from Uncle Kenneth's cluttered desk. From the wary expression on her face,

Dawn could tell she hadn't forgotten about the epi-
sode in Jennifer's room the other day.

"Is Jen upstairs?" Dawn asked her uncle.

"Yes, and I have a feeling she could use a little
cheering up," Uncle Kenneth said. "She didn't even
want to look at the bones we dug up on our last
archaeological expedition. I just brought them
home tonight."

Uncle Kenneth was always digging up old bones
and broken pots and plates and writing about them.
She didn't blame Jennifer one bit for not wanting to
look at his last find.

Dawn bounded up the stairs two at a time. "Jen!"
she called as she burst into the bedroom. "I've got
it! I know how to stop all the rumors going around
school!"

"You do?" Jennifer's voice floated out of the
hammock.

"Jen, I think there's going to be a little accident at
Barbie Davison's Halloween party. But luckily our
hostess's quick thinking is going to save the day."

Jennifer sat up abruptly, tipping the hammock
and almost falling out. "Dawn, what are you talking about?"

"Barbie," Dawn said. "She's going to be a hero. Or rather a heroine."

"After what she's gotten us into? Dawn, you're not making sense."

"Oh, yes I am." Dawn sank onto the edge of Jennifer's bed. She repeated the story Paul had told at dinner.

"What does Paul's basketball game have to do with Barbie?" Jennifer asked.

"The first thing Paul did was fumble the ball in front of everyone who thought he was magic. Once he stopped playing well, everyone began thinking they had been wrong about him. When Chuck Graham got to be the hero of the game—he was the one who started the guys thinking Paul could do magic in the first place—he took back everything he'd said."

"Just like Barbie was the one who got everyone at school thinking we're magical," Jennifer said. "Hmm, I'm starting to see what you've got in mind."

"I came up with a plan on the way over here." Dawn couldn't wait to share it with Jennifer. It was pretty clever, if she did say so herself. "It's going to involve some real acrobatics on your part, though," she added.

"That's okay," Jennifer said. "I can handle it. No matter what Barbie says, I didn't get my gymnastics trophy by using magic."

Dawn slowly explained the rest of her plan. She watched Jennifer's smile growing. "So, in the end," Dawn finished, "Barbie will be convinced that she was wrong about us. And so will everyone else."

"Dawn, you're a genius!" Jennifer exclaimed.

Dawn felt herself blushing. "I'm glad you like my idea."

"Like it? I love it!"

"Great." Dawn stretched out on Jennifer's bed. "Now that that's settled, all we have to do is decide what costumes we're going to wear." Dawn felt herself getting excited. Maybe this was going to be a fun Halloween party after all.

Nine

"Hey, careful, Dawn!" Jennifer said. "You keep stepping on my tail!" She reached behind her, and grabbed the long, black feather boa she'd sewn to the back of her black leotard and tights. Her hair was tucked into a black hood with little pointy ears attached to it, and she had penciled dark whiskers in between her nose and mouth.

"Ooops, sorry, Jen," Dawn said. "I can't see where my feet are going under this jack-o'-lantern." With the help of the special effects person at her parents' video company, Dawn had constructed a huge wire globe with a hole at the top for her head, a larger hole at the bottom for her legs, and two more holes where her arms stuck out. She had covered the contraption with bright orange fabric. Then she had used a black magic marker to draw the vertical lines of a pumpkin and to decorate the front with a Halloween jack-o'-lantern face. On her head, she wore a long green stocking cap for the stem.

She took a few more wobbly steps. It wasn't easy to walk around inside a giant pumpkin. She took up half of the sidewalk and her arms hung over the outside of the orange bubble. The shortcut through the narrow path behind Mrs. Holbrook's house was out of the question.

Dawn stepped into the street for a moment, to let a group of trick-or-treaters go by. She recognized most of them as sixth-graders from school. The pirate with the eye patch was Amy Page, Danny's little sister.

"Hi, Dawn! Hi, Jennifer!" Amy said. "Wow, Dawn, that's really a neat costume! Yours, too, Jennifer."

"Thanks," Dawn and Jennifer said at once. "You look great, yourself," Dawn added.

"You going to Barbie Davison's party?" Amy

asked. Dawn nodded, her chin bumping against the top of her pumpkin costume. "My brother's going, too. Wait till you see what he's wearing!"

Dawn felt her cheeks grow warm. She had been too embarrassed after the incident with Liza Martin even to talk to Danny again.

"Well, you guys, have fun. Don't eat too much candy," Dawn told Amy and her friends.

As Jennifer and she walked away, Dawn heard one of Amy's friends whispering loudly. "Aren't they those weird girls with the powers?"

Dawn sighed. She had been hearing comments like that for the last few days, and they still made her feel like the biggest freak at Crestfield Middle School. It sure would feel wonderful to put an end to all the rumors tonight.

Jennifer and she turned on to Barbie's street. They passed several houses decorated with paper skeletons and ghosts, and lighted jack-o'-lanterns in the window. Barbie's house was at the very end of the road, hidden behind a large stone wall with a wrought iron gate.

"Well, here goes nothing," Jennifer said. She and Dawn made their way up the slate walkway toward the three-story stone house. Barbie's suite of rooms took up the entire top floor.

"Look, Jen, that's where it's all going to happen." Dawn pointed at the tree that grew up past Barbie's private balcony. Her heart skipped a beat.

"Yeah, it's going to be a real show," Jennifer said excitedly as she rang the doorbell.

Barbie greeted them with her biggest smile. "Well, the most talked-about cousins of the year," she said brightly. "Hello, you two. What adorable costumes." Barbie was wearing a flared denim miniskirt and a Western-style shirt decorated with tiny rhinestones. Her blond hair spilled out from underneath a huge cowboy hat also studded with rhinestones around the band. She had topped off her outfit with a red bandanna and a large rope lasso.

Next to Barbie, Dawn felt like the Goodyear blimp in her orange bubble. But then she heard a familiar voice behind her on the front steps. "Wow! Who's that pumpkin in the totally outrageous costume? And who's that mysterious black cat with her?"

Dawn whirled around. "Megan? Is that really you?" Megan was dressed up as an alien. Under her coat, she was draped from head to toe with shiny silver fabric. Her freckled face was painted silver, too, and even her red hair had some kind of silver wash in it.

"None other," Megan answered, as Barbie let them all in. Dawn barely squeezed through the door frame.

"Well, you people just go on upstairs and have a wonderful time," Barbie said. "There's dancing in the front room, and we'll be bobbing for apples out back. Oh, and there are soft drinks and snacks, too. But, of course, people who can do what you two can do will certainly manage." Barbie let out a tinkly laugh, as if she had just said the funniest thing in the world.

Control yourself, Dawn told herself. *It's Barbie's house.* She forced a smile to match Barbie's. "I'm sure we'll all have a terrific time. Thank you."

Megan went off to leave her coat in the guest room, and Dawn and Jennifer decided to see what was happening in the front room. Loud music was playing, and a ghoul and a witch were dancing wildly. Nearby, Dawn saw Mark Potter, the cast on his arm sticking out from under a long black cape.

He wore a top hat on his head and was talking to a short, dark-haired ballerina—Liza Martin. Wilson Harris was over by the stereo—dressed up as a clown, of course.

"Hey, Dawn! You look good enough to eat!" He called to her. "Better make sure no one makes you into a pie."

As Wilson yelled out, Liza turned around. Dawn saw her take a look at their outfits. "Jennifer, I just knew you'd wear something spooky," she said loudly. "A black cat is so appropriate."

Jennifer gave Liza an icy stare. "Why don't you just button your lip, Liza?" she asked.

The color drained out of Liza's face. She immediately took off for a different part of the room. In her haste, she tripped over one of the ribbons from her slipper which had come untied.

"Gee, not a very graceful ballerina, is she?" Jennifer said.

Dawn reached out over her costume and managed to poke Jennifer in the ribs. "Jen," she said in a low voice, "we're supposed to be making people forget the rumors, not remember."

"I know, but I couldn't help it," Jennifer said.

"Listen, I'm going to sneak out to Barbie's balcony and scout out the scene." Jennifer grinned eagerly, and the whiskers penciled on her face crinkled up.

"You want me to come?"

"Better not. With that big orange thing on, you might attract too much attention from the people coming up the driveway. I don't want anyone to catch me planning this. You stay here and have fun."

"Okay," Dawn said. But she wasn't sure how much fun she could have in a room full of people who thought she was strange and eerie. When she saw Liza Martin eyeing her suspiciously from across the room, Dawn decided to hunt for the refreshment table.

Along with the chips and dip, she found Danny Page. He was impossible to miss. The second Dawn squeezed her pumpkin costume through the door to the next room, she spotted him—towering head and body above all the other kids! At first, all she could see was his flannel shirt way up above Chuck Graham's head. Danny's hair was tucked into a knitted cap, and he was holding a fake ax in one hand. As Chuck moved out of the way, Dawn could see the huge pants that didn't quite cover the bottom of the stilts Danny was on.

"Wow!" she said to the ghost next to her. "What a great costume. I didn't know Danny could walk on stilts."

"Yeah, he's Paul Bunyan," the ghost answered in Janie Simon's nasal voice. Dawn held in a little giggle. This was a first—a ghost who was probably more scared of people than they were of her. "Hey, your costume's pretty cool, too," Janie said.

"Thanks."

All of a sudden, Janie gave a little gasp from under her sheet, as if she had remembered something. "Oh, um, excuse me, but I want to say hi to someone over there." She gestured vaguely and took off like a runner at the starting pistol.

Dawn bit her lip. *Barbie's rumor at work again,* she thought. She couldn't wait for everyone to start treating her like a normal eighth-grader again.

She sighed and looked up at Danny once more. He noticed her and gave a big wave. "Look! It's the magic pumpkin!"

Dawn could feel herself getting hot with embarrassment under her costume. She was starting to wish she had never heard the word "magic." She gave a little half-wave back, and slunk away. Or as close to slinking as she could manage inside a huge, orange pumpkin.

"Hey, Dawn, watch where you're going!" Cindy Mitchell said. She had on a party hat and funny glasses.

"Oops, sorry, Cindy. Did I bump into you?"

"Yes, you did. You know, if you had used your ESP, you would have known I was here."

"Cindy, I don't have ESP," Dawn said hotly. But Cindy didn't look convinced. Dawn crossed her fingers and hoped that Cindy would feel differently by the end of the night. Cindy and everyone else at Crestfield Middle School.

"Me-ee-oow?" Jennifer hopped up on the railing of Barbie's balcony and arched her back.

"Ooo, Jennifer, be careful!" Marthe Geisbond pleaded. Marthe had come to the party dressed as a hippie. Dawn thought she looked pretty much the same as usual, though she had on a few extra scarves and bangly bracelets, and she had painted a flower on one cheek.

"Hey, don't worry, Marthe," Wilson Harris said. "A cat has nine lives."

"Wilson, be serious for once in your life," Marthe said. "She could really hurt herself up there."

Dawn watched Jennifer prowl along on all fours. She knew she could use her magic to bail Jennifer out if she absolutely had to. Still, it was a little scary to watch her cousin crawl to the edge of the balcony railing. It was a long way down.

"Marthe, there's nothing to worry about," Sue Flagg said. "She can always save herself by magic."

"I don't believe that for a second," Gary Elwood said. Gary had a computer screen painted on the front of his T-shirt, and a computer keyboard on the back. Strips of computer paper hung out of all his pants pockets. It was the perfect costume for him.

Jennifer looked out at the leaves on the giant oak tree that towered over Barbie's balcony. "Mmm, I see a little birdy in that tree who looks purr-fectly appetizing," Jennifer said. There was laughter from the growing crowd of kids on the balcony.

The laughter changed to gasps of shock and

fright, as Jennifer squatted on her haunches and then suddenly leaped into midair. She gave a loud hiss as her hands and feet left the balcony railing. Her feather boa tail danced in the air.

Dawn's breath caught in her throat.

Jennifer raised her arms and grabbed a thick branch of the oak tree. As she pulled herself up onto the limb, Dawn felt herself breathe normally again. The terrified gasps turned to murmurs of appreciation.

"Wow, maybe she can teach us cheerleaders some of her tricks," said Wendy Hiller. Wendy had hundreds of purple and yellow streamers hanging from the neck of her T-shirt, almost down to the ground. Leave it to the Crestfield Cougars' biggest fan to come as a human pom-pom in the school colors, Dawn thought.

"Wendy, I'm afraid you have to be magical to do those tricks," said Barbie, stepping up to the part of the balcony nearest the tree. She squeezed in next to Mark Potter. Perfect, Dawn thought with glee. This was just what Jennifer and she had been waiting for.

Jennifer stood up and walked out to the middle

of the branch. "Yum-yum, little tweety bird," she called out. "I'm going to have you for dinner with my favorite sauce." She grabbed the next limb above her, and did several chin-ups.

"Barbie, make her come out of that tree," Marthe Geisbond pleaded. "You don't want any accidents at your party."

But Barbie just smiled even more brightly than usual. "Marthe, normally I'd be very nervous. But since it's Jennifer Nicholson, I don't think we have to worry. It's awfully nice of her to put on such a good show for my guests, though."

Jennifer balanced on the branch on one leg. Then she balanced on the other. "Oh, tweety!" she called. Dawn watched her making an exaggerated search for the imaginary bird.

"Ah, you're down there, my little feathered friend," she said. A roar of surprise went up as she jumped down to another thick branch a few feet below the one she was on. The crowd of kids surged forward to watch her, then let out a gasp as only one of her slippered feet landed solidly. The other one slipped off the branch, sending her plummeting off her perch.

Dawn's scream stuck in her throat. She got ready to arch her eyebrow.

But Jennifer managed to hook one leg onto the branch. As she hung there, upside down, her arms and one leg dangling in space, her glance met Dawn's. Dawn could see the tiny, mischievous glimmer in her cousin's eyes. Jennifer had fallen on purpose. Now it was Dawn's turn to play her part.

"Jennifer! Pull yourself up!" she yelled out.

Jennifer made struggling motions. "I can't! I'm starting to slip!"

"Somebody help her!" Dawn screamed.

"How?" Marthe Geisbond cried back. "She's too far down. No one can reach her!"

Dawn turned to Barbie. "Quick! Your lasso! Lower it down to her!"

Barbie laughed. "Don't you think it would be more interesting for Jennifer to give us a magic show? I'm sure we'd all like to see how she gets out of this. Or how you get her out, Dawn."

"Barbie, this is no time for jokes about magic," Dawn said. "Jennifer needs your help!"

"Yeah, come on, Barbie," Danny Page called out.

But even Danny's encouragement wasn't enough. Barbie didn't budge. Dawn felt a jolt of nervousness. Barbie wasn't going for the bait. "Please," Dawn tried again. "You've got to do something."

"You cousins," Barbie said. "I don't understand why you're so shy about showing your friends at school what you can really—"

"Dawn!" Jennifer screamed.

Dawn gave a start of fear. There was real fright in her cousin's voice this time. When she turned back toward Jennifer, she could see that her leg was beginning to tremble with the strain of holding the branch for so long.

"Barbie!" Dawn shouted again. If Barbie didn't act right this second, Dawn was going to have to use her magic to save Jennifer. Right in front of everybody in the eighth grade! And then she'd never live down Barbie's rumor.

Barbie stood there, smiling infuriatingly.

"Dawn!" Jennifer yelled again. "This is for real! Please!"

Dawn felt her pulse pounding. She looked at Barbie. Barbie stood her ground. Then she looked

back at Jennifer. She could see her cousin's leg starting to give way. She had no choice. Dawn arched
her eyebrow.

But Jennifer kept slipping. Dawn arched it again.
And again. Jennifer's arm flailed as if she were trying to grab on to something. Anything. Dawn kept
arching her eyebrow, but it was useless.

Oh, my stars! It can't be! Dawn's blood ran cold.
My powers are out!

"Dawn!" Jennifer screamed again. "You've got to
do something!"

"I can't!" Dawn shrieked.

Suddenly, she heard something whistle past her.
Barbie's lasso! "Catch, Jennifer!" Barbie shouted.

Dawn watched as the lasso shot out over the
thick limb that Jennifer was slipping from. The
loop hung down, only inches away from Jennifer's
gloved fingers. Her hands grabbed wildly, and she
couldn't get a grip on the rope.

But just as Jennifer's leg lost contact with the
branch, she managed to close her hands around the
loop. Barbie lurched forward under the pull of Jennifer's weight.

Instantly, Mark Potter shot forward as if he were

going after a tackle. He grabbed onto Barbie's end of the lasso with his good hand. Even one-armed, he was strong enough to steady the rope.

Jennifer hung from the other end, her knuckles white as she clutched the rope with all her strength. This time she didn't attempt any chin-ups or fancy stunts. Terror was plain on her face.

"Hold on, Jennifer, we're going to lower you down to the next branch," Mark shouted. He and Barbie let out the lasso little by little, until Jennifer's feet were brushing it. But it was a much thinner limb than the one she'd fallen from, and her legs were shaking so much, she couldn't get her balance.

"Come on, Jen," Dawn encouraged. "You're almost safe."

"You can do it!" Wendy Hiller cheered her on.

Finally, Jennifer got her feet solidly on the branch. Dawn held her breath as her cousin let go of the lasso and clasped the limb above her. She inched toward the trunk of the tree. And then, very, very carefully, she climbed back up to the balcony.

Dawn didn't let her breath back out until Jennifer stood right in front of her. Jennifer's knees were shaking, and one leg of her tights was in shreds. Underneath, the skin on the back of her leg was badly scraped. But she was safe!

Dawn burst into tears of relief.

"I'd hug you, but I think I'd squash your costume," Jennifer joked weakly.

"Oh, Jen! You could have been killed!"

Suddenly, Dawn was aware of someone else sobbing next to her. She turned around. Barbie!

"I-I could have been too late," Barbie cried. Her phony smile was nowhere to be seen. "I really believed my own crazy story. But then I saw how scared you both were . . ." She sniffled back her tears. "I owe you both an enormous apology. To think of what might have happened . . ."

Dawn felt a wave of sympathy for Barbie. She reached out over her costume and patted Barbie on the shoulder. "Jennifer is fine, Barbie, thanks to that fast lasso of yours. Sure is a good thing you were blue ribbon material at that dude ranch."

Barbie's smile was back. For once it was genuine. "If Jennifer had gotten hurt I would never have forgiven myself. I don't know how I ever could have gotten it into my head that you two have supernatural powers. I mean, I was sure I saw all kinds of—well, never mind. It must have been my imagination. What a dumb idea."

Dawn and Jennifer traded private smiles. Their plan had worked!

Ten

"When I saw you hanging there, I realized how horrible I'd feel if anything happened to you," Kitty DeVries was telling Jennifer. Rather than part with the Cleveland Indians cap she always wore, Kitty had added the rest of the team uniform and come to the party as a baseball star.

"Does that mean you want to sit with me at lunch again?" Jennifer said happily. She had refused to leave the party when Dawn had suggested that maybe she should go home and rest. Instead, she had simply cut the tattered portion of her tights away with a pair of scissors and washed her scratched, bruised leg.

Dawn stood by the refreshment table and watched her cousin. Jennifer's near-accident was getting her just as much attention as her fake powers had. And the attention was of a much better kind.

"Wow! All those moves you did in the tree were amazing," Wendy Hiller said.

"Weren't you terrified?" Janie Simon asked. She didn't seem the least bit afraid of Dawn or Jennifer anymore.

"Well, maybe a little," Jennifer answered.

"Boy, you should be a TV stuntperson, or something." Only Wanda Jackson, dressed as a Vulcan with pointy ears, could manage to relate everything to television.

"You know, Jennifer," Donna Lee said, "you may not have powers, but you do a really good job of reading those tarot cards. I've been getting a ton of baby-sitting jobs."

"I guess you're a good babysitter, Donna," Jennifer said. "The cards don't have anything to do with it."

Dawn helped herself to some peanuts and raisins. She was the one who had planned the whole scene out on the balcony, and yet Jennifer was getting all the attention. It didn't seem very fair.

"Um, excuse me," a voice said, way above her head. Dawn whirled around and looked up—way up—at Danny Page. "Do you think maybe you'd like to dance?" he asked. "I mean, as much as I can dance on these. It's more like moving my weight from one stilt to the other. But if you don't mind . . ."

"It's okay," Dawn said. "I'm not exactly Miss Graceful in this costume, either. I can't even sit down."

"Does that mean you'll dance with me?" Danny asked.

Dawn laughed. "We're going to look pretty funny out on the floor, for sure."

Danny led the way into the other room. At the edge of the dance floor, Danny looked down into Dawn's eyes. "I'm glad you wanted to dance. I thought you'd been avoiding me."

"Really?" Dawn said.

"Yeah, ever since that day you ran away when Liza Martin—" His voice trailed off. As Dawn looked up at him, she saw a look of confusion on his face.

What if the rumors weren't dead after all? she wondered with a sinking feeling.

"—when Liza Martin was so nasty," Danny finished. "You know, I was so mad at her for the things she was saying that I almost thought I saw her lips buttoned."

"You're kidding!" Dawn hoped she sounded surprised enough.

"But that's impossible, isn't it?" Danny looked down at her intently. Dawn felt his blue eyes holding hers. For a moment, she wondered if Danny still suspected the truth.

"Well, what do you think?" she asked nervously.

"I think it's about as impossible as a magic pumpkin." Danny laughed. The slow song coming out of the speakers ended, and a fast dancing rhythm began. "And now, if the Great Pumpkin would care to dance with Paul Bunyan . . ."

"Wendy Hiller?" Jennifer exclaimed. "I can't believe it!" She kicked a twig that had fallen onto the sidewalk. "And after all the trouble I went to, performing all those dumb tricks and learning to read those stupid tarot cards."

"Jen, I'm really sorry," Dawn said. "I know how much you wanted to be Homecoming Queen."

"I just don't understand how it happened." Jennifer's voice wavered unhappily. "How did everyone at Crestfield Middle School wind up voting for Wendy?"

"Not everyone," Dawn reminded her cousin. "The Hawk said it was a really close vote." Mr. Hawkins, the principal, had announced the vote at the noon assembly.

"But Wendy Hiller?"

"I know. I still keep picturing you in your grandmother's dress with the Homecoming crown on your head," Dawn said. "I wish it were going to be like that." The girls turned off of School Street and headed toward Dawn's house.

"Yeah, maybe if I hadn't talked you into conjuring up a matching outfit and all that stuff, you would have had some power left to help me get elected," Jennifer said.

"Jen, look, you know how much I was hoping you would win, but even if I had double my usual powers, it wouldn't have been fair to throw the vote. Maybe people picked Wendy for a good reason."

"What reason?"

"Homecoming is a celebration for the football team, Jen, and Wendy's the Cougars' most dedicated cheerleader and fan."

"You mean, you think Wendy's a better choice, too? Boy, of all the traitors. Maybe I *shouldn't* be going home with you this afternoon."

"Jennifer Nicholson!" exclaimed Dawn. "I did *not* say I thought Wendy would be a better Homecoming Queen. I just meant that you have to respect the votes of the kids at school."

"I do?"

"Yeah, you do. Aren't you learning about the democratic process in Social Studies class? Besides, you wouldn't have really wanted to win by magic instead of a fair vote, would you?"

"Doesn't sound so bad," Jennifer said.

Dawn laughed. "Honestly, Jen. Where are your principles?"

"Maybe they fell out of that tree at Barbie's when I was hanging upside down," Jennifer said with a straight face.

Dawn knew this was a good sign. Jennifer hadn't lost her sense of humor. She'd get over her disappointment before long. "Anyway, Jen, didn't you get enough attention this week to last you a while?" Dawn asked.

Jennifer shrugged.

"Come on. 'Fess up," Dawn said. "Isn't it nice to be plain old Jennifer Nicholson again?"

Jennifer stopped in her tracks and folded her arms. "Dawn, Jennifer Nicholson is never just 'plain old.'"

Dawn grinned. "Oh, right. Excuse me. What I meant to say is, isn't it nice to be extraordinary, wonderful, terrific Jennifer Nicholson again?"

"Well, when you put it that way . . ."

"And how about being friends with Kitty again?" Dawn prompted.

"Yeah, that's the best part of all this magician stuff being over," Jennifer admitted. "I guess real friends are worth a lot more than the instant ones I was trying to make with all my tricks. Even if I didn't have enough to get me elected Homecoming Queen," she added.

Dawn didn't give her cousin another chance to start feeling sorry for herself again. "Hey, speaking of tricks, I've been meaning to ask you how that empty can trick works."

Jennifer gave her a mysterious smile. "You should know better than that, Dawn. A magician never tells."

Dawn smiled back. Her cousin was one hundred percent right. That was one lesson Dawn had definitely learned this week. A magician never tells her secrets.

ABOUT THE AUTHOR

EVE BECKER discovered her own magical powers in eighth grade when she got her teachers to believe her homework excuses. She has been inventing stories ever since. She has lived in Spain and France, but her permanent residence is in New York City with her husband, William Liebeskind, a painter. In her free time, she enjoys sports, dance, and traveling.

Shop at home
for quality childrens books
and save money, too.

Now you can order books for the whole family from Bantam's latest catalog of hundreds of titles, including many fine children's books. And this special offer gives you the opportunity to purchase a Bantam book for only 50¢. Here's how:

By ordering any five books at the regular price per order, you can also choose any other single book listed (up to a $5.95 value) for just 50¢. Some restrictions do apply, so for further details send for Bantam's listing of titles today!